## Author's Note:

This children's book is dedicated to all the essential workers that are helping businesses and industries stay open for all Americans to maintain a basic way of life. Not forgetting the parents and educators who are working from home, educating children during the COVID-19 pandemic with the hope of returning to normalcy.

# Foreword

As an educator, writing this book was a milestone achievement in these uncertain times of the COVID-19 pandemic. I found hope and comfort from the words of my parents to share the story of children and adults impacted by the current situation. The fictional characters were used to share the experiences of children and the rapid changes in schools across the United States. I have learned that working together and following the recommendations of health professionals will change the trajectory of COVID-19 and save lives.

On one gloomy day in Bayside Queens, Selwyn, QB, Grace, and Chico were on their way to Public School 411 Elementary. Selwyn rushed into the building to read the morning news. He was reminded to follow the rules.

Selwyn headed off to the principal's room, past the janitor, sweeping with his broom, filled with excitement for the news of the day, wondering just what his morning speech would say.

Selwyn met with Principal Jones to review the morning news. But Principal Jones looked very sad, and quickly said "Good morning, P.S. 411. School will be closed tomorrow. A letter will be sent home with each kid today."

Selwyn was confused and wondered just what the letter would say.

Selwyn returned to class, feeling the blues because he did not read the morning news. Grace, Chico, and QB said, "We expected you to read the news. What did the letter say?"

Selwyn replied, "We will get the letter by the end of the day. We can just get through our lessons right now, and whatever it is, we will manage somehow."

Miss Crabtree began teaching math facts and vocabulary. The kids were thinking about the morning news and began to worry. After completing the math lesson, the children were ready for recess time. There were so many clouds and no sun to shine.

During recess, Selwyn was reminded about the morning news. The kids were feeling blue. Grace and QB said, "Selwyn, we have a question for you. What did the letter say? Why do we have to stay away?"

Selwyn replied, "Our parents will read the letter and share the news. Those are the rules."

Miss Crabtree gave students the take-home letters. "The writing on the letters are big and bold which makes us feel sad and cold," said QB, Chico, and Grace.

Selwyn replied, "Our parents will read and explain the letters to us."

The Bayside Bunch delivered the letter from Principal Jones. Parents shared the news that the school will be closed for three weeks. We follow the rules. There is a dangerous virus called COVID-19 that has affected Queens.

Not returning to school made Selwyn scream. Selwyn said, "I am going to miss sharing the morning news."

"Those are the rules." replied his parents. Selwyn said, "Quarantined in Queens. So that is the news that the letter outlined?"

So that is what happened to the Bayside Bunch. All were staying home, staying safe, no friends there at lunch. Selwyn missed reading the news, but he missed his friends most of all. Selwyn wished there was a way to keep reading the news and seeing all his friends, without breaking the rules.

With their phones and computers, the gang had a way to keep in touch every day. All Selwyn had to do was persuade the school that using the internet didn't break any rule. So he asked his parents to talk to his teacher and suggest that they could use the internet to bring the whole school together.

Selwyn's mom spoke to Miss Crabtree to explain the idea and see what she thought. "It's a great idea," said Miss Crabtree, "but I need to make sure everyone is safe online. I will check things out, and then we will see."

Then Selwyn's parents received a phone call from Miss Crabtree. She wanted to check-in and offer support to the family.

"Thank you for checking on me. I miss being in school, talking to my friends, and reading the morning news. Now I am sad and feeling the blues," said Selwyn.

Miss Crabtree replied, "I have an idea. I will talk to Principal Jones; it could bring you some cheer."

The following day, Selwyn received a telephone call from Principal Jones. "I hope you are well and ready to share the school news," said Principal Jones.

Selwyn took one breath and was no longer blue. "What do you mean?" he asked.

"Miss Crabtree came up with a great idea. You will share the morning news using a program called Kaboom," said Principal Jones.

Selwyn replied, "Okay. I can share the morning news from my room."

Selwyn logged onto Kaboom from a desk in his room. There appeared to be images of smiling faces that filled the room.

The children cheered without fear.

"Selwyn, I feel like I haven't seen you in a year," said Grace.

As he saw all his friends, Selwyn started to smile and then got ready to read his first news for a while.

"Our parents shared that there is a 6 feet rule. We hope it will help us return to school," said Selwyn.

"But there is more that Principal Jones's letter taught us:

- Wash hands with soap and water for 20 seconds
- Cover your cough and sneeze with a tissue and throw it away
- Avoid touching your eyes, nose, and mouth
- Avoid contact with people who are sick
- Stay at home if you are sick
- Clean and disinfect touched areas frequently

"If we can do all this and obey the rules, we can be out of our homes and back into school," said Selwyn.

The next day, Selwyn logged onto his computer at eight, so he wouldn't be late. He quickly shared the morning news. Of course, the children were all still worried about going back to school.

Then Miss Crabtree joined Kaboom to talk about their concerns about returning to school.

Selwyn said, "Our lives have to change, which is very strange."

Miss Crabtree shared some helpful suggestions for motivating the Bayside Bunch. She said, "Read for 20 minutes each night or have someone read to you."

Selwyn replied, "I have been writing about my experiences out of school."

QB, Chico, Grace said, "That's so cool."

The children are excited to share their feelings about being out of school with Miss Crabtree.

• "My dad is playing goalie from the fridge. I was on the way to the kitchen for a slice of cheese. A loud voice said, 'Freeze.' Dad said that we are eating too many snacks. We had to fall back," said QB.

• Grace said, "I have practiced for the school play all year. Will I ever get my day?"

• "I miss sharing the morning news at school. I am beginning to feel the blues," said Selwyn.

• "At P.S. 411, I am a shy kid. Not returning to school makes me cry," said Chico.

Miss Crabtree replied, "I miss all of you, and I look forward to seeing you soon."

The Bayside Bunch are enjoying family time in Queens. Returning to school is becoming one big dream.

Families in Bayside are keeping their children engaged. More than three weeks of no school, they will become afraid.

After a long day of activities, Selwyn sets his alarm clock for school. He is happy to see the Bayside Bunch and read the morning news. Selwyn is no longer singing the blues. Life is different, but he is no longer afraid.

The Bayside Bunch are on their way to school. Selwyn ran into the building past Miss Crabtree's classroom, which wasn't cool.

Selwyn began reading the morning news. "It's great to be back at school with my friends. We share a circle that never ends. Three weeks of no school passed through my brain and was driving me insane. Principal Jones and Miss Crabtree called to check in with us. They are caring and kind, always looking to help us every chance they can find," said Selwyn.

Selwyn returned to class and received a big cheer. Chico, Grace, QB said, "Selwyn, you are the most popular kid of the year." The Bayside Bunch was excited to return; they quickly realized there was so much to learn. They couldn't wait for the bells to ring for recess. The playground was their favorite place to de-stress.

After an exciting day in school, the Bayside Bunch returned home. Grace, Chico, and QB said, "The adults in our school are cool."

Selwyn replied, "A school is a happy place where the adults understand me."

"When will we return to school? I've still got so much to learn," said Selwyn.

# COVID-19 Strategy for Children

Dear Parents,

Lasirena Books believes that creating a daily journal is a great strategy to de-stress children during the current COVID-19 period.

Getting each child to write down their thoughts and memories from each day in their very own journal can be therapeutic and provide some insight into how the child is feeling. For instance, journaling can also involve art, based on the fact that drawing pictures of their cat or doing whatever activity they did helps them focus on positive things. If you can, organize this with other parents so that children can share their stories with friends and reduce the feeling of isolation that is perhaps the most challenging struggle at this time.

We have provided some writing prompts to assist children in their journal entries:

- My favorite way to spend the day is...
- What does friendship mean to me?
- I enjoy going to school because...
- My favorite color is...

For additional information and your queries about journaling activities with your children, please feel free to contact us at lasirenabooks01@yahoo.com.

Thanks,
Lasirena Books

# Keep Children Healthy During the COVID-19 Pandemic

According to the Center for Disease Control (CDC), children do not appear to be at higher risk for COVID-19 than adults. While some children and infants have been sick with COVID-19, adults make up most of the known cases to date.

## Watch your child for any signs of COVID-19 illness

COVID-19 can look different in different people. For many people, being sick with COVID-19 would be a little bit like having the flu. People can get a fever, cough, or have a hard time taking deep breaths. Most people who have gotten COVID-19 have not gotten very sick. Only a small group of people who get it have had more serious problems.

CDC and partners are investigating cases of multisystem inflammatory syndrome in children (MIS-C) associated with COVID-19. Learn more about COVID-19 and multisystem inflammatory syndrome in children (MIS-C).

## Keep children healthy

Teach and reinforce everyday preventive actions
- Parents and caretakers play an important role in teaching children to wash their hands. Explain that hand-washing can keep them healthy and stop the virus from spreading to others.
- Be a good role model—if you wash your hands often, they're more likely to do the same.
- Make handwashing a family activity.
- Learn more about what you can do to protect children.

Keeping Children Healthy during the COVID-19 Outbreak. (2020, June 14).
National Center for Immunization and Respiratory Diseases (NCIRD), Division of Viral Diseases.

# About the Author

**Dr. Unseld Robinson** has served as a school administrator in New York for more than 20 years. He is a graduate of the New York City Public School System. Dr. Robinson has spent many years mentoring students and developing caring, trusting, and bonding relationships with them. He currently resides in Buffalo, New York.

Dr. Robinson is the author of
*The Bayside Bunch:
Go See the Principal!*
It has been used in various schools and after care programs to develop positive relationships between children and adults.

For more information
visit **www.lasirenabooks.com**
Instagram: @lasirenabooks
Facebook: @lasirenabooks

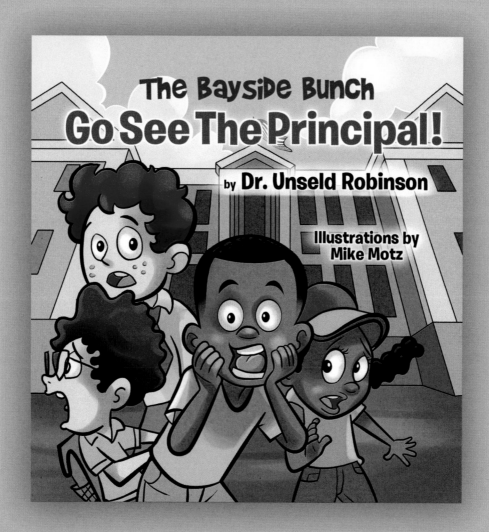

# Helpful Tips for Parents

Helping children relax not only helps them cope with the situation better, but it can be a great help for you too! Here are three things you can do to keep children relaxed in such an unfamiliar situation:

• **Talk to them about what is happening** – They know things have changed. Don't try and hide it from them. They will be more relaxed if they feel you are not hiding anything.

• **Take time to breathe** – Get the children to grab their favorite cuddly toy, sit down in a comfy spot, and breathe slowly in and out. See if they can focus on being quiet. It's great for the children and you.

• **Try some art** – Get the paints out and let your children express themselves. Visual arts have long been linked with resilience to stress, and for children, it allows them to get any emotions they are struggling with onto the paper, helping them relax.

Made in the USA
Monee, IL
01 February 2021